spend the night at Steve's?

Please?

Spot, what

are you taking with you?

It's a good thing next

I live door, Spot...

What are you looking at,

Spot?

Watch out for the flowers, Spot!

Here comes your mum, Spot.

Hi, Mum!

What do you want?

My mum's calling

us, Spot.

What was in

Did you